Note to parents, carers and teachers

Read it yourself is a series of modern stories, favourite characters and traditional tales written in a simple way for children who are learning to read. The books can be read independently or as part of a guided reading session.

Each book is carefully structured to include many high-frequency words vital for first reading. The sentences on each page are supported closely by pictures to help with understanding, and to offer lively details to talk about.

The books are graded into four levels that progressively introduce wider vocabulary and longer stories as a reader's ability and confidence grows.

Ideas for use

- Although your child will now be progressing towards silent, independent reading, let her know that your help and encouragement is always available.

- Developing readers can be concentrating so hard on the words that they sometimes don't fully grasp the meaning of what they're reading. Answering the puzzle questions on pages 46 and 47 will help with understanding.

For more information and advice on Read it yourself and book banding, visit www.ladybird.com/readityourself

Book
Band
9

Level 4 is ideal for children who are ready to read longer stories with a wider vocabulary and are eager to start reading independently.

Special features:

Clear type

Full, exciting story

Richer, more varied vocabulary

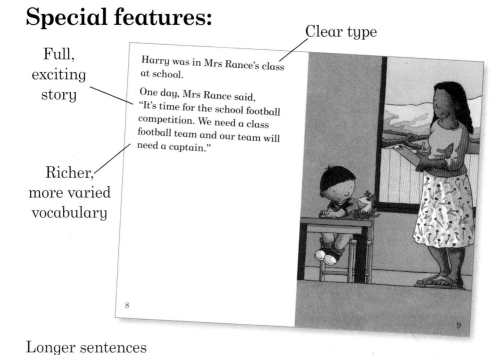

Harry was in Mrs Rance's class at school.

One day, Mrs Rance said, "It's time for the school football competition. We need a class football team and our team will need a captain."

8

9

Longer sentences

After school, Harry and the rest of his team went to Mr Oakley's field to practise.

The children ran about everywhere, but they got in each other's way.

14

15

Detailed illustrations to capture the imagination

Educational Consultant: Geraldine Taylor
Book Banding Consultant: Kate Ruttle

First published by David & Charles Children's books 1999
Text adapted by Lorraine Horsley

A catalogue record for this book is available from the British Library

This edition published by Ladybird Books Ltd
80 Strand, London, WC2R 0RL
A Penguin Company

001

Text copyright © Ian Whybrow, 2013
Illustrations copyright © Adrian Reynolds, 1999

The moral right of the author and illustrator has been asserted.

Ladybird, Read It Yourself and the Ladybird Logo are registered or
unregistered trademarks of Ladybird Books Limited.

ISBN: 978-0-72327-534-3

Printed in China

Harry and the Dinosaurs United

written by Ian Whybrow
illustrated by Adrian Reynolds

Harry and his dinosaurs went everywhere together.

When Harry went to the shops, the dinosaurs went to the shops.

When Harry went out to play, the dinosaurs went out to play.

And when Harry went to school, the dinosaurs went to school, too.

Harry was in Mrs Rance's class at school.

One day, Mrs Rance said, "It's time for the school football competition. We need a class football team and our team will need a captain."

Mrs Rance picked Harry to be the team captain. He was very excited.

The dinosaurs all wanted to play, so Harry picked them first. Then he picked the children for the rest of the team.

At play time, Harry and the dinosaurs talked about which position they wanted to play.

Triceratops and Tyrannosaurus wanted to play in goal.

Pterodactyl wanted to play on the wing.

After school, Harry and the rest of his team went to Mr Oakley's field to practise.

The children ran about everywhere, but they got in one another's way.

Then Harry's big sister, Sam, turned up.

"Right!" she said. "All of you can play against me!"

The dinosaurs all ran after Sam,
but they could not catch her.
When they were all puffed out,
she ran past them and scored.

"Your team is rubbish!" said Sam. "I can beat them on my own. You will never win the competition!"

Harry was so cross, he kicked the ball hard into Mr Oakley's field.

Nan and Mr Oakley came to see what the ball was doing in his field.

"Sam said our football team is rubbish," said Harry.

"You're not rubbish," said Nan, "you just have to practise."

"That's right," said Mr Oakley. "Come back again and you can practise playing football against me and my old friends."

So the next day, Harry and the rest of his team came back to Mr Oakley's field.

"Here we are, Harry," said Mr Oakley. "We may look as old as your dinosaurs, but we can play football as well as you can."

The dinosaurs were worried about playing. "We don't want to be rubbish," they said.

"Don't be worried, my dinosaurs," said Harry. "If you don't want to play, you can be our mascotasauruses! We will have a Triceratops mascotasaurus, a Tyrannosaurus mascotasaurus and a Pterodactyl mascotasaurus."

Harry knew that the way to win was to play together as a team.

"Right," he said. "Don't all run after the ball and get puffed out. Stay in position or run into a space and call for a pass."

On the day of the competition, Harry and the dinosaurs were excited but worried.

The children in the other team were older and bigger than them.

Harry and his team each got
a mascotasaurus and ran on
to the football field.

"Come on, Dinosaurs United!"
they roared.

Harry's team played very well,
but at half time they were two
goals down.

"Time for a team talk,"
said Harry.

"Come on!" said Harry. "Play together and we can win!"

And the mascotasauruses
all roared,
"Let's all get excited
for Dinosaurs United!"

In the second half, Harry and his friends played just like a real football team.

They stayed in position and passed the ball.

And with just seconds to go, they scored two goals.

Then Harry ran into a space.

He knew what to do. He called
for the ball. "Pass it! Pass it!"

Harry kicked the ball as hard as he could.

It went right in the top corner...

GOAL!

Harry had scored the winner.
Dinosaurs United had won!

On the way home, Mr Oakley said to Nan, "You can't beat us old dinosaurs, can you?"

"Not when we play as a team!" said Harry.

How much do you remember about the story of Harry and the Dinosaurs United? Answer these questions and find out!

- Who does Mrs Rance pick to be team captain?

- Where do Harry and his team go to practise?

- Why does Harry get cross?

- Who do Harry and his team practise against?

- Who wins the football competition?

Unjumble these words to make words from the story, then match them to the correct pictures.

Hyrar

Rm Oylake

Sma

Msr Recan

Nna

Read it yourself with Ladybird

Tick the books you've read!

For more confident readers who can read simple stories with help.

Level 3

YOU won't like this present as much as I DO!

The Elves and the Shoemaker

☐　☐

Hansel and Gretel

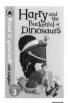
Harry and the Bucketful of Dinosaurs

Jack and the Beanstalk

Furi on Music Island

Poppet Stows Away

Rapunzel

The Red Knight

☐　☐　☐　☐　☐　☐　☐

Longer stories for more independent, fluent readers.

Level 4

I am Inventing an INVENTION

Harry and the Dinosaurs United

☐　☐

Heidi

Katsuma and the Art Thief

Luvli and the Glump-a-tron

The Pied Piper of Hamelin

Sam and the Robots

Snow White and the Seven Dwarfs

The Wizard of Oz

☐　☐　☐　☐　☐　☐　☐